A Window On My World

Robert Edward Conner

VANTAGE PRESS
New York

FIRST EDITION

Copyright © 1996 by Robert Edward Conner

Published by Vantage Press, Inc.
516 West 34th Street, New York, New York 10001

Manufactured in the United States of America
ISBN: 0-533-11462-4

Library of Congress Catalog Card No.: 95-90126

0 9 8 7 6 5 4 3 2 1

In loving memory
to my will-o'-the-wisp

Contents

A Window On My World

In Quest of A Snow-blind Author

1995

I sense the snowflake's gentle touch;
    it starts me reminiscing
about a poem I once read
    wherein every ninth letter was missing.

'Twould seem a bit odd,
    but with apologies to no man,
the author named his masterpiece
    "R me Of The Snowman."

It concerned a young lad
    with no meanness in mind,
whose aim, swift and true,
    left that author snow-blind.

Now, go find that poem,
    unleash your mind's fetters,
and learn ye the secret
    of those missing ninth letters.

Hearth's Desire

1984

Smoldering embers,
    springs gone by warm my winter.
      My heart remembers.

Peek-a-Boo!

1995

When I was 'bout six and she was 'bout four
    her family happened to move next door.
Most houses in those days were separated
    by tall wooden fences, but we were fated
to meet, and to love, and I'm happy to say
    that it came about in a cute kind of way:

I never had met her, then one day I heard
    a lilting laugh like a tiny bird,
and I followed its trail to a point real low
    where only the wee folk like us could go,
and I peeked through a knothole, and what did I see
    but a sparkling blue eye peeking back at me!

Small Wonder!

1941

I've oft seen a beautiful rainbow
 arching high across misty skies,
and many a glorious sunset
 has pleased these critical eyes.

I've caught the aroma and beauty
 of a freshly budding rose,
and thrilled at the sight of a tiny child
 asleep in sweet repose.

O'er lofty snow-capped mountain peaks
 I've watched a new dawn breaking,
and known a peace and solitude
 that set my heart to aching.

I've walked 'neath the stars on winter nights
 while the world lay quiet and still,
and I've watched the play of the Northern Lights
 from a most convenient hill.

My soul has been stirred by the haunting strains
 of heavenly melodies,
and I've been kissed by a vagrant breeze
 as it frolicked 'mongst the trees.

Yet, of all the wonders of this great world
 I have found 'neath the heavens above,
the wonder that captures my innermost heart
 is the wonder of your love.

My Own Petard

1950

Not a tumble would she give me
    and it made my poor heart sore,
so I tried my best to win her—
    being spurned, I loved the more.

To prove her how much I cared,
    fine presents I did shower,
sent notes of love both day and night
    and 'phoned her every hour.

With all the wiles long known to man—
    and some I invented—I wooed her;
'tho every ploy was met with scorn,
    my one-track love pursued her,

'Til, one fine day, she said "I do,"
    and since then life has taught me
that, far from pursuing, I'd been pursued,
    and my will-o'-the-wisp had caught me!

Sounds of Life

1965

Pitter-patter of falling rain,
   mournful wail of a distant train,
      an airplane in its lonely flight,
         tramp steamer whistling in the night,

the hurried tap of girls' high heels,
   the creak and groan of wagon wheels,
      a stream that murmurs on its way,
      a rooster's crow to start your day,

owl's hoot that echoes through the dell,
   shipboard, "eight bells and all's well,"
      old hound dog baying at the moon,
      a haunting gypsy violin tune,

drone of bees heard midst the flowers,
   a carillon that chimes the hours,
      windsong that plays among the trees,
       child's bedside prayer upon her knees,

stray cat meowing in the dark,
   a puppy practising its bark,
      a fledgling squawking in its nest,
      spanked newborn howling in protest,

marching feet and a muted drum,
   thunder as tho' your time had come,
      train wheels rolling, clickety-clack,
      a crossing bell that answers back,

school bell that calls the child to class,
   church bell that calls devout to Mass,
      strange noise that wakes you from a dream,
      the tea kettle, letting off some steam,

the creaking of an old porch swing,
    and, in it, voices whispering,
        snoring of someone deep in sleep,
            croaking of frogs, knee deep, knee deep.

Myriad sounds have pleased my ear,
    but there is one I hold most dear;
        her voice, which never fails to start
            a thump-thump-thumping in my heart.

First Anniversary

1946

One month ago I knelt with you
  and realized a dream come true,
    your sweet voice whispering "I do."

And as you spoke a wondrous light
  shone 'round us, as a halo might,
    and your hand gripped mine, oh, so tight.

Then in my heart I breathed a prayer
  that God might always keep this pair
    as close as we were, kneeling there
      one month ago.

Doctor's Vigil

1953

From out the stygian void my rival came,
    but I perceived him nigh and made all speed
to beat the devil at his fiendish game,
    to keep him from committing his foul deed.

There in the darkened room the battle raged,
    and dawn had brushed aside the cloak of night
before my adversary disengaged
    his fierce grip and conceded me the fight.

No, not the fight . . . I've only won a round.
    Death stalks each mortal 'til he's under ground.

The Parting

1969

No more to see the light of love
    that sparkled in your eye,
no more to hold you in my arms
    and kiss the tears you'd cry,
no more to hear your lips profess
    your love for me, for I
have held you close for one last time
    and heard your last good-bye.

Acoustical Error

1969

Often, in my lonely plight,
    a voice screams loudly to the night
    a name I've dearly known.
The voice, familiar to my ears,
    so poignant, plaintive, filled with tears,
    I find to be my own.

I listen, rapt, as hopes rebound,
    then hear a most horrendous sound:
    the thunderous, thundering,
    heart and soul sundering,
    ear-splitting sound of
    silence.

Enigma

1969

Would that this muted pen I lift
    in some enchanted manner might
be endowed with the magic gift
    to sense my ev'ry thought and write,
to pour out on the barren page
    emotions I cannot control,
the conflicts that within me rage,
    the torment that besets my soul.

Cradle Song

1985

The while the body earns the tomb
    the soul yearns toward another mark:
      the refuge of the mother's womb,
        the haven of that warm wet dark.

Perchance to Dream

1994

One side of my bed gets slept in,
    as it has for twenty-four years.
One side of my bed was wept in,
    when Death came, and with it, my tears.

For twenty-three years our love was a flame
    that kindled the fire of our mating game,
but ever since then, as I've grown old,
    this bed of mine has grown mighty cold.

For twenty-four years the very most
    to warm my bed has been my love's ghost;
a new love, perhaps, a new warmth might weave,
    but I never could get that ghost to leave.

So I'll stick with this bed 'til I trade it in
    for a grave where my true love has waited within
through those twenty-four years since her life did stop,
    and we'll grow so much closer, with me on top,

      until, as we planned it, in a few thousand years
      our bones will have mingled with our love and our tears.

Opus 174—A Grave Affair

Little girl lost, lovely wraith in the mist
    of memories come back to haunt me,
      of hopes that once lived deep within my heart,
      of dreams returning to taunt me.
Ghost from my past with a tear in your eye,
    is it you who are lost? Or am I?

Colleen Elizabeth

1994

A tiny blossom was created,
lighter still than any feather,
from a mixture of love
and sweet william
and heather.

April 21, 1994

1994

I watched it draw near
with a smile on my face;
with an effort
I somehow contrived
not to show my impatience
with its leisurely pace
as my great-granddaughter's
third birthday arrived.

Harbingers

1984

Warming winds that flow
    to the tow'ring mountaintop
      quench their thirst in snow.

Rivulets descend,
    mating and multiplying . . .
      spring is 'round the bend.

Pike's Peek

1994

The mountain shed
its snow-white shroud
and thrust its head
above the cloud
to scan the countryside,
and then
slipped down beneath
the cloud
again.

's No Use

1995

It's snowing right now in Albuquerque town,
    but I must tell you, to my sorrow,
that it makes no sense for snow to come down . . .
    it will disappear by tomorrow.

Now, don't go thinking snow's not a regular here . . .
    I remember it snowing one day last year!

A Taste of Winter

1972

'Neath a low'ring sky
   snowcaps rim the valley green
      . . . cream on Key lime pie!

Harvest

1972

Sparkling bright dewdrops,
    nectar reaped by morning's sun;
    dawn's light finds new crops.

Thunderstorm Footnote

1972

Blankets tucked in
  at the foot of the bed
    so tight I can't pull them
    up over my head.

Dammed Nuisance

1972

This storm, by gosh, is
    overflowing river banks
      . . . and my galoshes.

"Corn" Bread

1972

In the hot bake pan
   a golden mound of butter
     now lies, shortening.

Fall Guys

1972

Box kites in a bunch
   collapsing into the sea
      . . . pelicans at lunch.

Golf

1972

My drives are weak as they can be,
    my chip shots much too strong,
but still, this game's my cup of tea:
    my putt just went Oolong!

Contentment
with a Capital "F"

1994

I keep on hopin',
    keep on wishin'—
with baited breath
    I keep on fishin'.

Play Ball!

1975

Sports types, reasonin'
  TV fare needs spice,
    welcome baseball seasonin'.

Heart Murmur

1938

"He has no heart," my critics say,
    but oh, how wrong those fools!
I know enough to love and leave
    before some maid's heart cools
ere mine, and I am left alone
    to grieve and yearn and smart.

Oh, no, I've learned! I want no more
    of Love's scars on my heart!

Bric-a-Brac

1938

I placed you on a pedestal,
    alabaster quite divine,
and dwelt in Seventh Heaven
    with the knowledge you were mine.
You said none else could win your love
    but then there came a day
you toppled from your pedestal
    and became common clay.

Target of Opportunity

1975

My heart has been cleft;
    ambidextrous Cupid's darts
      pierce me right and left.

Then, to my intense delight,
    o'er and o'er and o'er again
      pierce me left and right.

Tacit Assent

1986

Should I pat you on a buttock,
    I beg you not to speak.
Do what peace-loving females should!
    Please! Turn the other cheek.

The Eyes Have It

1986

I watched her little derriere
    swish by me as I tarried.
I yearned to pet that little lass . . .
    and so, the motion carried.

The Hot Young Miss
and
the Merry Old Soul

You climbed into my bedroom
    with the first faint flush of dawn
and crept where I lay naked
    as the day that I was born.
You kissed my hair, my cheeks, my lips,
    my shoulders and each breast
while ever so soft light fingers
    my hips and thighs caressed.

With your touch my waking body
    more hotly then did burn,
and when you probed between my legs
    I had to toss and turn
'til at last I could stand no more
    but had to rise and run
to draw the blinds and shut you out.
    You'd grown too hot, old Sun!

Apple Con Puta

1992

The reason that Adam,
   I firmly believe,
let Eve get at him
   was, he was nigh Eve.

Food for Thought

1986

Which of her legs is loveliest?
    The question does intrigue me,
and this enigma I'll resolve
    although it should fatigue me.

I'll view each limb objectively,
    with fine detail I'll screen them;
my head will then bend to its task
    and make up its mind between them.

On We?

1992

If our romance falters
    because our love alters,
      whose fault can it
        possibly be?

The onus is on *us*
    if boredom's upon us
      (or would you rather say
        it's ennui?)

D. O. M.

1955

When all's said and done,
    which brought me more fun?
. . . the limbs I explored,
climbing trees as a child,
or the limbs I explored
    when girls first drove me wild?

If I still had my druthers
    climbing girls or a tree,
I think I'd still climb
    those young girls. Yessiree!

Shall Do! Shall Do!

1995

The things women do
    shall always excite me,
shall tease me and please me
    and always delight me.

The thing my love shall do
    shall forever be
the most love-giving thing
    in the world to me.

Now, hidden within
    those lines up above,
delve deeply and find
    a wondrous object of love.

A Passage of Arms

1981

Poised for a battle to the bitter end,
    each legion waits the onslaught of the foe,
alert for openings Kind Fate may lend,
    resigned to yield if Cruel Fate wills so;
and in each van a rank of men does stand,
    first to be sacrificed if need must be,
pawns at the mercy of their liege's hand,
    resolved to lead the way to victory.

Then, bringing up the rear in staunch array,
    regarding the encounter as mere sport
while yet determined they shall win the day,
    the King and Queen, and members of the Court.

And there it comes, the move that starts the war:
    White's simplest opening, Pawn to King four!

A Matter of Some Antics

1995

"C'est la vie!" (That's life!), under my breath I'd say
    when some well-laid plan went awry,
which brings to my mind a bygone day*
    when my new amanuensis, with a twinkling eye,
said, "You're making no sense when you whisper 'Se la ví',
    so this lesson you should not forget:
you've been saying, in Spanish, 'I saw yours!,'
    and you *haven't* seen mine . . . yet!"

*Circa 1960: . . . and, darn you, Irene, I never did!

42

Gourmet, Dining

1995

I stopped by an eatery,
    a favorite "take-out" of mine,
whose menus (food and waitresses)
    border on the divine,
for either could be delicious
    with candles and wine.
Then, to satisfy my appetites,
    although I loved them all,
I finally came home
    with a spicy meat-a-ball!

Table the Question

1994

If someone calls you
    a procrastinator,
tell him you'd prefer
    being called a cunctator.

Don't look it up now—
    you can do that later.

Tex Hex On New Mex Sex?

1995

A Texas-sized moon rides high in my sky,
while the Man In The Moon has a gleam in his eye
as though he knows a secret I ought to know!
WHAT'S A TEXAS MOON DOING HERE IN NEW MEXICO?

R me of the Snowman

A   flurry   of   snowballs
    from   a   boy's   eager   f st
came   fly ng   at   me
    and   t   seemed   he   had   m ssed;
then   h s   a m   spo led   my   v ew
    for,   to   my   great   surpr se,
h s   m ss les   sped   true
    and   he   knocked   out   my   's.

Hindsight

1983

A little behind,
   astronomers find it ringed.
     You bet! Uranus!

Powered Flight*

1944

In turn the restless engines spit
  and cough and growl, like animals
    that find their slumbering disturbed,
     but soon emit a docile purr
      as by their master's hand they're curbed.

Now, thrust aloft in headlong flight
  I watch the pageant of the night
    unfold.

*Reciprocating engines, of course.

Ad Astra

1995

Yon firmament presents a wondrous sight,
    arching high in the midnight sky
with its trillions of stars in majestic flight,
    twinkling firelfies soaring on high.
'Tis said that most stars are spinning in pairs
    in a show well worth paying to see,
but I feel those performers are just putting on airs
    in a setting where no air should be.
'Tis also said CASPER, one of the TWINS,
    is not just a single star,
but are three separate pairs, all twirling around,
    sky's smoothest performers by far.
And some "fireflies" don't twinkle at all,
    but are lit by reflection from stars;
we have called those "planets", and given them names
    like JUPITER, SATURN AND MARS.
There's a total of nine in that great beyond,
    of varying distance and girth,
including just one on which life can be found,
    this one that we're standing on: EARTH!
I counted those stars one fine summer's night—
    as a child, hasn't everyone?
and I've learned that each star is a sun, somehow:
    I wonder how God got that done?

Nepotism in High Places

A job opened up
    in the kingdom of the Lord
        . . . and went to His Son.

Sole in Purgatory

1975

The angel spoke:
   "Wait 'til you're called."
    We waited, hosts of us.

Eons have passed,
   those hosts long gone
    . . . I think I've missed the bus.

Profundity

1973

"Satan," I asked, "how came ye here
    to rule the nether spaces?"

"Acrophobia," he replied.
    "I've this G.D. fear of high places!"

But Few Are Chosen

1973

Dear Lord, I do appreciate the fact
    that you have chosen me to live with you,
that you regard my ev'ry earthly act
    as what you've wished each mortal soul would do.

Your heaven is so vast and beautiful,
    and 'tho ungrateful now I might appear,
I long for one female as dutiful,
    'Cause, Lord, I've been so G.D. lonely here.

The Happy Hour

1987

From four to six they're gathered there,
    unhurried, relaxed, no worries or care,
a cosmopolitan crowd, you'd agree,
    as universal a group as could be.

No prejudice, no color bar, no caste . . .
    inequality? A thing of the past . . .
a Tower of Babel? No, there is not
    one indication of the polyglot.

These representatives of various nations
    share common language; thus, conversations,
quite contrary to waxing abundant,
    are of necessity quite redundant.

The mutual experience they'd shared
    comes once in a lifetime, 'tho some had dared
to evidence a disinclination
    toward a rather abrupt invitation.

And you will also, I shouldn't wonder,
    when *you* are invited four to six feet under!

The "Good Old Days"

1995

The "turn of the century" brought on the close
    of an era that lives on in song and in prose.
Let us drift back in fancy to those golden years
    when just reminiscing brought laughter and tears;
then we'll turn back the clock to that 'Gay Nineties' time
    when the word "gay" meant "happy," and a smiling
        "L'chaim!"
was a toast to your health, and two beers cost a dime,
    and folks, in simple honesty and boundless good cheer
      called a spade a spade, and called a queer a queer!

Hinc Ilae Lacrimae*

1992

Researching down the ages,
    this truism I have found:
Man made God in *his* image.
    'Twas *not* the other way 'round.

*Latin: Hence These Tears.